CONTENTS

When lightning struck Barry Allen's lab, the young forensic scientist was bathed in chemicals. Soon after, his body underwent an extraordinary change that turned him into the fastest man alive. He could race up buildings, run on water and create sonic booms with his incredible speed. Realizing his new abilities could be used for good, Barry set out to protect his home town of Central City.

He became . . .

The FLASH ™

CHAPTER 1

EXPLOSIVE DIVERSIONS

BRRRRRRIIIIIIIIIING!

An alarm rang out as a helmeted robber burst from the bank. He carried a large, green duffel bag as he dashed across the road.

"Look out!" the robber shouted. "Get out of my way!"

Citizens dived left and right as the crook ran towards a motorbike and hopped on.

VROOM!

With the bag strapped to the seat behind him, the criminal pulled out into traffic and sped away.

The motorbike roared through the busy streets. It zigzagged around cars and trucks as if they were standing still. As the bank robber zipped around a tight corner, he hit an opening in the traffic and poured on the speed. Little did he know a red blur was trailing him – and closing in fast.

Just as the bank robber thought he was home free, The Flash appeared and ran alongside him.

"I have to hand it to you," the Scarlet Speedster said with a grin. "If you're going to commit a crime in Central City, you have to be fast."

The robber shook his head in disbelief. He sped up, but The Flash easily kept pace with him.

"I'm just saying that the motorbike was a really great choice," the hero continued. "But I'm sorry to tell you, it's just not fast enough."

The Flash dropped back for a moment. Then he reappeared on the other side of the motorbike. The hero held the large duffel bag in his arms.

"I've got the money," The Flash said with a shrug. "So you might as well give up now. Even the fastest motorbike is way slower than me."

The Flash's eyes widened in surprise when the robber only laughed.

VROOM! VROOM!

The hero was even more surprised when two more speeding motorbikes joined the race. They were each driven by helmeted riders and had identical green duffel bags strapped behind them.

The Flash cocked his head slightly. "Okay, that's new."

The two new motorbikes pulled ahead. They each zipped down different side streets. The first crook sped away as the hero skidded to a stop to look in the bag.

BEEP·BEEP·BEEP·BEEP·BEEP!

The bag beeped in the hero's hands. The Flash opened the bag to see a device counting down.

"Oh, boy," The Flash said as he poured on the speed once again. "I'd better head for the river."

When he reached the centre of the river's bridge, the hero tossed the bundle over the railing. As the bag hit the water, it exploded.

POOF!

A giant smoke bomb released a towering grey cloud that hung harmlessly over the river. The Flash was gone before the smoke cleared. He raced down the busy streets. He had to catch up with the real bank robber.

The Scarlet Speedster spotted one of the crooks racing through a junction. The hero was so fast, he didn't need to stop for the red light. He dodged the crossing traffic before the drivers knew he was there.

The Flash caught up to the crook and took a different approach. This time, he snatched up both the bag *and* the driver. He held them up as the motorbike continued forward without them. It fell over and slid to a stop.

"Now, let's try this again," The Flash said.

The helmeted crook shook his head. The hero's mouth fell open as he held the bag up to his ear.

BEEP·BEEP·BEEP·BEEP·BEEP!

"Ah, come on!" The Flash said as he dropped the criminal. He clutched the bag in both hands and ran away.

The hero didn't have time to make it back to the river. He also didn't want this smoke bomb to go off in the middle of a busy street. He had to get rid of it some other way. Luckily, a tall skyscraper loomed just ahead.

The Flash increased his speed as he raced towards the building. When he reached it, he didn't slow down. The hero ran so fast that he was able to travel up the side of the building.

The hero zoomed faster and faster as he neared the top of the skyscraper. Then, at the last second, he flung the bag as hard as he could.

WHOOSH!

The Flash stopped on the roof and watched the bag shoot into the sky.

POOOOF! The smoke bomb exploded, creating a huge, billowing plume high above Central City.

"Third time's the charm," The Flash said as he sped back down the building. He had to pick up the trail of the last motorbike.

When the hero hit the street, he started criss-crossing the city as fast as possible. Unless the crook with the real bag of money had gone into hiding, The Flash was sure to find him.

The Scarlet Speedster finally spotted his target. The bank robber's motorbike darted through heavy traffic as he entered a tunnel. Lines of cars and trucks filed in after him.

The Flash ran towards the tunnel's entrance in a blur of red. "It's going to get crowded in there really fast," he said. "Unless . . ."

When The Flash entered the tunnel, he took a hard right. Keeping up his speed, he raced up the side of the tunnel wall. He kept going until he sped along the ceiling, above all the vehicles.

Up ahead, the crook on the motorbike looked over his shoulder. He didn't spot the hero running above him. The Flash shot past the crook and then dropped to the ground. The criminal turned back and saw the super hero, but it was too late.

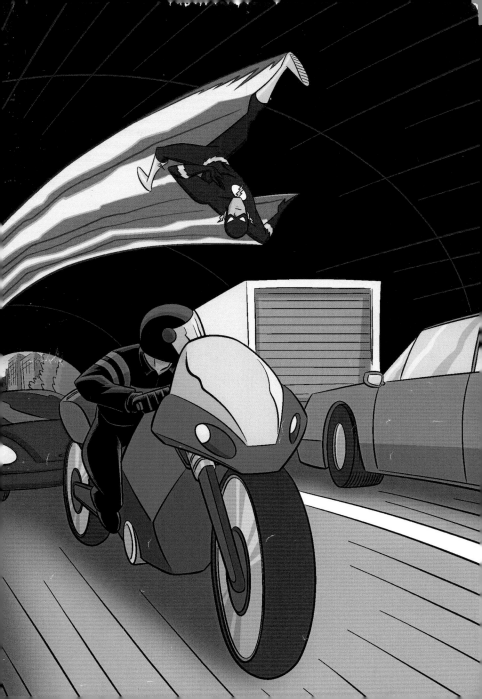

With lightning speed, The Flash reached out and grabbed the motorbike's hand brake. The bike skidded to a stop and the robber flew over the handlebars. Cars and trucks stopped around them as the crook tumbled across the road.

The Flash snatched up the duffel bag and peeked inside. It was stuffed full of cash.

"Just checking," the hero said with a sigh of relief.

The Flash zipped over to the fallen crook and jerked him to his feet. He pulled off the robber's helmet. A frightened man stared back at him.

"That was a nice trick with the decoys," The Flash said. "But did you and your friends really think those smoke bombs would slow me down?"

"It . . . it wasn't our idea," stammered the man. "This guy paid us to rob the bank. Gave us the smoke bombs and everything."

"Who?" asked The Flash.

The man shook his head. "I don't know. We never met in person."

The Flash hoisted the man under one arm and the duffel bag under the other. He raced out of the tunnel towards the police station.

"I know someone at the police station who can find out who was behind all this," The Flash said.

* * *

On a mountaintop high above Central City, a lone figure climbed the side of a tall metal structure. He pulled out a wrench from his tool belt.

From this viewpoint, the figure had seen the first smoke bomb explode over the river. He had chuckled when he spotted the second plume of smoke high above the city. His plan had worked perfectly. The Flash had been kept busy while he put the finishing touches on his latest project.

The man laughed as he tightened the last bolt. There was no way Central City's super hero could stop him now.

CHAPTER 2

THE COMING STORM

The next morning, Barry Allen crept up the back stairs of the police station. When he was The Flash, Barry was The Fastest Man Alive. Unfortunately, as himself, Barry Allen was constantly late. He did his best to sneak into work without being caught by . . .

Captain Frye, who was waiting for him in the crime lab. "Late again, Allen," Frye said, crossing his arms.

"Sorry, Captain," Barry said. He held up a small paper bag. "I brought doughnuts, though. That's still a cop thing, right?"

The captain shook his head and glared at Barry for a moment. Then he snatched the bag out of his hand. "You're lucky you're our top criminal scientist." He jutted a thumb towards the work table. "Now, get to work. Those smoke bomb pieces aren't going to examine themselves."

As the captain left, Barry checked out the electronic shards and bits of cardboard and plastic on the table. The police had collected several smoke bomb fragments from the river. It was Barry's job to see if the pieces contained any clues that would tell him who made the smoke bombs. If they discovered that, they would find out who hired the crooks to rob the bank.

Barry switched on a small television and then began examining smoke bomb bits. He often had the local news on in the background while he worked. On the screen, the news anchor, Cliff Stevens, tapped on a coffee mug with a pencil as he gave out the latest headlines.

"And now, let's see what's in store for the weather," Stevens said. "Let's go to Central City's own weatherman, Phil Yonkos."

"I'll be standing in for Phil today," said an oddly familiar voice. "And I'm here to tell you . . . there's some stormy weather ahead."

Barry looked up at the television and froze when he saw the person on the screen. A man with short grey hair was dressed in a green and yellow costume. A small mask covered his eyes and a wide grin stretched across his face.

Barry recognized the villain instantly. It was one of The Flash's most cunning enemies, Mark Mardon – better known as the Weather Wizard.

"Hello, Central City," the criminal continued. "I have a special announcement for you . . . my retirement."

"What?!" Barry exclaimed as he set down his lab tools. "I can't believe it!"

"I bet that's hard to believe," the Weather Wizard said, his grin stretching wider. "But it's true! I'll blow out of your city for good as soon as you pay me . . ." He put a finger to his chin. "Let's see . . . what's a nice, round number?" He snapped his fingers. "Twenty million dollars! I've even set up a special website, all ready for your donations."

"That's crazy," Barry said to himself.

The Weather Wizard chuckled. "I know, I know. It probably seems like a crazy idea. But if you really think so, maybe you should look out your window." He crossed his arms. "Go ahead. I'll wait."

Barry ran to the window and saw a darkening sky. Thunder rumbled and lightning streaked across the clouds.

"You see, Central City is in for the storm of the century," the criminal continued. "I've even surrounded the city with a fog so thick no super hero can get through to save you."

RUMMMMMMMBLE!

The building shook beneath Barry's feet as the thunder grew louder.

"Of course there's The Flash," the Weather Wizard continued with a chuckle. "But come on. Is he faster than lightning?"

KRAK!

A blinding bolt of lightning struck just outside the building. Windows shattered and frigid air blew in. Icy rain sprayed into the lab while the wind swept up papers in a mini whirlwind.

The Weather Wizard is going to tear the city apart, Barry thought. *I need to act fast.*

Barry raised his hand and opened his special ring. His red uniform sprang out of the tiny ring and grew larger and larger. In the blink of an eye, Barry Allen changed into The Flash.

The speedster leapt out of the window and ran down the side of the building. He hit the pavement and sped down the street. He had to get to the news station and stop the Weather Wizard.

Just before The Flash could really pour on the speed, he spotted a group of people in trouble up ahead. Hail pelted the street all around them.

Normally, a little hail wouldn't be an emergency, but these balls of ice were the size of small watermelons. The hail dented car roofs and smashed through windscreens.

The Flash zigzagged through the street. He moved so fast that he darted between the balls of ice before they hit the ground. The hero snatched up citizens and dropped them off in doorways and under awnings. Then he pulled people out of cars before their vehicles were smashed around them.

Once he had moved everyone to safety, The Flash took off towards the news station. He turned a corner and stopped short in the middle of a junction.

"Oh, man," The Flash said as he took in the scene.

He saw the worst kind of weather in every direction. A blizzard blew in from the north. Sheets of rain rolled in from the south. Bolts of lightning terrorized the east, and a tornado whirled in the west.

"This really is the storm of the century," he said.

CHAPTER 3

DANGEROUSLY HIGH WINDS

WHOOSH!

I need to take down the biggest threat first, The Flash thought as he zoomed towards the tornado.

The giant twister was so powerful it churned up the road as it thundered down the city street. It sucked up parked cars and hurled them around in its spinning funnel.

Luckily, the Scarlet Speedster had dealt with massive tornadoes before. All he had to do was run around the twister in the opposite direction. He would run fast enough to create a strong wind of his own and unravel the dangerous tornado.

The Flash didn't waste any time. He zipped to the base of the twister and began circling it at incredible speed.

SWOOSH! SWOOSH! SWOOSH!

With a few more loops, he would have this thing broken up in no time.

"Help!" shouted a distant voice.

The Flash looked up and caught a glimpse of a woman trapped inside a small car. The tornado lifted it higher and higher.

The tornado will have to wait, he thought. *If I stop it now, that car will drop like a rock.*

The hero skidded to a stop and began running in the opposite direction. He quickly matched and then surpassed the tornado's speed. He zoomed so fast that he was able to jump onto the wreckage churned up by the raging twister.

The hero sped up a broken light pole and then leapt onto the bonnet of an empty car. From there, he pushed off and landed on a loose door. The Flash rode the door like a surfboard as it spun him higher and higher into the sky.

"Whoa!" The Flash shouted as he ducked. A large postbox whipped over his head and smashed into another car.

The Flash glanced up and spotted the woman's car. He had to get to it before the twister crashed it into another car or flung it free.

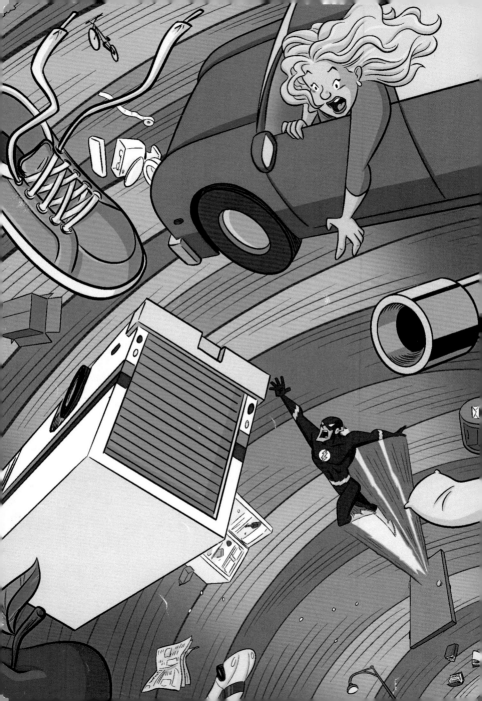

The Flash crouched and then sprang towards an old truck. He barely made it, catching the bumper with both hands. The hero pulled himself up and then scrambled onto the roof. From there, he leapt onto another car, and then another.

Now the woman's car was right above him. Unfortunately, the small vehicle circled the tornado faster and faster. He would have to time his next jump just right.

The Flash waited for the car to come around again. *Here goes nothing*, he thought as he pushed off with all of his might and soared through the air.

WHOOSH! THUNK!

The Scarlet Speedster shot through the open window and dropped down into the passenger seat. The frightened woman stared at him in disbelief.

"Having a little car trouble?" The Flash asked jokingly. "Don't worry. I'll get you out of here."

The hero tried to push open the car door, but the powerful winds slammed it shut again.

"Okay," the hero said, "we're not going out that way." He glanced around the small car, stopping at the roof. "What do you think about owning a convertible?"

The Flash didn't give the woman a chance to answer. His hands were a blur as he punched a line through the front of the car's ceiling. Once he was finished, the wind caught the roof. It peeled back like the lid on a sardine tin.

The Flash lifted the woman out of the seat. "Okay, this is our stop."

The woman clenched her eyes shut as the Scarlet Speedster held her tight and sprang through the hole in the roof. The car flew away as the hero kicked off.

The Flash dropped onto another vehicle and ran across its roof. He leapt off and then sped across half a billboard, another two cars and then a park bench. The hero took a final leap and landed on the pavement.

"Now let's get you to safety," The Flash said. In the blink of an eye, he raced down the street and dropped the woman off three blocks away.

"Thank you," she said with a weak smile.

"Better get inside, ma'am," the hero said. "I don't know how long these storms will last." He darted back towards the tornado. "But this twister is toast!"

Then The Flash ran around the giant funnel in the opposite direction. The hero was a blur of red as he circled it faster and faster and faster.

Soon, the speedster created heavy winds of his own. They rose higher and higher, finally unravelling the tornado. The hero stopped circling but had to dodge falling wreckage.

BAM! BOOM! KRASH!

Several empty cars smashed to the ground around him.

While the hero caught his breath, he noticed a display of televisions in a nearby shop window. He zipped over for a closer look and noticed that they all showed the same thing – Weather Wizard's running total of how much money he had collected.

"Well, I'll be," The Flash muttered.

It turned out that the citizens of Central City were willing to pay to make the storms go away. The criminal was nearly halfway to his goal.

The Flash tightened his lips. He wasn't going to let the crook get away with this. He took off in a blur, heading towards the television station. Thick droplets of rain pelted him as he zoomed onwards.

As the Scarlet Speedster zipped through a junction, he glanced down the cross street. "No way," The Flash said as he slid to a stop.

He sped back to the junction to see a flash flood pouring down the avenue. Frantic men and women ran from the approaching wall of water.

"I guess the TV station will have to wait," the speedster said as he spun around.

The Flash rocketed down the street and rescued citizens from the thundering flood. He scooped up a person with each arm before running down side streets and dropping them off where they'd be safe. Then he dashed back to get more.

The hero deposited some citizens far enough away that they wouldn't be swept up by the flood. But since there were so many, he had to place some of them on top of tall delivery trucks, just above the raging waters. Zipping back and forth, The Flash kept ahead of the wall of water and cleared the citizens from its path.

I can't keep this up forever, he thought. *I have to find a way to end this flood completely.*

As he turned to face the churning water, his mind raced for ways to stop it.

Should I dig a really big trench with my super-speed? he thought. *Should I race in a circle, like I did with the tornado? Maybe create a funnel that sucks the water up and out of the city?*

Suddenly a familiar voice interrupted his thoughts. "Well, look who it is!"

The Flash spun around to see one of his biggest enemies standing before him. The man wore a blue and white costume with a fur-trimmed hood. It was Captain Cold. The super-villain pointed his cold gun right at The Flash.

CHAPTER 4

TEMPERATURE DROP

"Listen, Cold," The Flash told him. "This isn't really the best time –"

"Duck!" ordered Captain Cold.

The Flash darted to one side as the criminal fired his weapon.

BZZZT!

A thick stream of ice exploded from the cold gun and shot past the hero.

CRACK!

The blast hit the approaching wave, and ice spread out over the water. Loud crackling filled the air as the wall of water froze solid.

"What? Why are you helping me?" asked The Flash. "I don't get it." He was thoroughly confused.

Captain Cold shoved the cold gun back into its holster. He chuckled to himself as he approached The Flash.

"Look, I know I often work with the Weather Wizard, but I had nothing to do with any of this," the criminal explained. "None of the Rogues are involved." The Rogues were a group of crooks that both Captain Cold and the Weather Wizard were a part of.

"Okay," The Flash said suspiciously. "I guess I'll just have to take your word for it."

The villain shrugged. "Hey, if that giant goofball takes everybody's money, what's left for the rest of us to steal, huh?"

The Flash scratched his head. "I guess you have a point there."

The criminal pointed at him. "So the question is, big super hero, what are you going to do about it?"

"I'll tell you what I'm going to do," the Scarlet Speedster said, jutting a thumb over his shoulder. "I'm going to the television station to put an end to this mayhem, once and for all."

"Yeah," said Captain Cold. "About that. You're going to hit this big blizzard along the way." He raised both hands. "I had nothing to do with that. Just saying."

WHOOSH!

The Flash turned and ran as fast as he could. He had barely gone five blocks when he saw that Captain Cold had told the truth. Several feet of snow slowed his passage and thick snowflakes filled the air. The speedster had to work twice as hard to plough through the thick snow.

"I don't understand how the Weather Wizard can create all these storms at one time," The Flash said as he slogged his way through drifting snow. "He's never been this powerful before."

As the speedster neared the station, he heard muffled cries for help. That's when he noticed several suspicious mounds of snow all around him. The Flash reached into the nearest pile and felt around.

"There's a person trapped in here!" The Flash exclaimed.

SWOOSH! SWOOSH! SWOOSH! SWOOSH!

The hero's arms became a red blur as he brushed away the snow. Soon, a shivering man in a police uniform was revealed.

"Th-th-thanks, F-F-Flash," said the chilled police officer. "The s-s-storm came on so f-f-fast, I d-d-didn't have e-e-enough time to t-t-take cover."

The Flash jutted a thumb at the other mounds of snow. "It looks like you're not the only one," he said. "Help me dig out the other human ice lollies."

The Flash and the police officer moved to the other mounds of snow. As they worked together, several shivering citizens were revealed. Once the last person was uncovered, The Flash zipped towards the street. The puzzled people watched as he dug around in the snow.

"Come on," the speedster said. "There has to be one around here somewhere."

After a bit more searching, The Flash found what he was looking for. He spun around in a red blur, flinging snow everywhere. When he stopped, he stood beside a small fire hydrant.

The police officer moved closer. "No offence there, Flash, but the last thing we need around here is water."

"I agree," said The Flash. He crouched and rubbed the hydrant with both hands. "But these people need to warm up fast."

SHHH! SHHH! SHHH!

The speedster's hands became a blur as he rubbed the hydrant faster and faster. He moved so quickly that the metal became warmer and warmer.

As The Flash cranked up the speed, the fire hydrant finally glowed red hot. The freezing people crowded around the scorching fire hydrant to warm themselves.

"Thanks again, Flash," said the police officer. He held his hands over the glowing hydrant.

"That should thaw you out until I put an end to this crazy weather," The Flash said.

Without any more distractions, the hero ran to the nearby news building and hurried inside. He dashed up the stairs and burst into the television studio. He spotted the familiar setting he usually watched every morning as he worked in his lab. Except now, the newscasters didn't look happy. They looked tired and worn down. Every view screen in the studio showed the Weather Wizard's ransom tally.

The Flash ran up to Cliff Stevens. "Where is he?" the hero asked. "Where is the Weather Wizard?"

The news anchor shrugged and glanced around. "He's not here, that's for sure. He took over our television signal from somewhere else."

Stevens took a nervous drink from his coffee cup. "We don't know where he is."

"I think I know where the Weather Wizard is operating," said a woman's voice.

The Flash turned to see a young woman wearing a headset and holding a clipboard on the opposite side of the studio. He zipped up to her so fast the papers on her clipboard ruffled in the wind.

"What do you mean?" asked the Scarlet Speedster.

"The Weather Wizard is broadcasting on all channels," the woman explained. "There's only one place near Central City powerful enough for that."

The woman moved to a window and pointed east. "He has to be using our main antenna. If it weren't for the blizzard, you could see it up there on the mountain."

"That makes perfect sense," The Flash said. "Good work."

The Scarlet Speedster dashed out of the studio and back onto the street. He pushed through the thick blizzard and headed due east. Along the way, he saw his city being hit by all kinds of weather: rain, hail, sleet and snow. Luckily, he didn't spot anyone else in trouble. He could finally concentrate on taking down the Weather Wizard once and for all.

When he reached the edge of the city, The Fastest Man Alive was stopped in his tracks. As promised, the villain had encircled the city with a thick fog.

As The Flash dashed into the thick haze, he realized he was running blind.

CHAPTER 5

FASTER THAN LIGHTNING

This is going to take a while, The Flash thought as he jogged through the heavy fog. He wasn't used to moving so slowly. He felt as if turtles could move faster than he was right now.

But if I use my super-speed, I could slam into something or someone, he thought. *Luckily, you don't need superpowers to be a super hero.*

The Flash couldn't see through the thick fog, but he could use his other senses. He reached out and felt tree trunks around him. He heard birds chirping above him. And he smelled fresh pine needles. He even felt the ground slope upwards.

I may be moving at a snail's pace, The Flash thought as he made his way up the mountain, just east of the city. *But I know I'm heading in the right direction.*

As the climb grew steeper, The Flash heard voices ahead. He picked up the pace and soon found himself on a narrow hiking trail. He followed the trail higher and the voices grew louder.

"Katie!" a man shouted.

"Honey, can you hear us?!" a woman called through the fog.

As he neared the voices, two hikers came into view. A man and woman stood together on the trail. Both looked relieved when they spotted The Flash.

"Thank goodness you're here," the woman said to the hero. "We can't find our daughter anywhere."

"Katie was running just ahead of us when the fog rolled in," the man said. "But before we could catch up with her, the fog became so thick we got separated."

Normally, The Flash could run every trail on the mountain in less than a few seconds. But in this heavy fog, he was as helpless as they were.

"It's best you stay here," the hero told them. "Once I take care of this fog, I'll find your daughter. I promise."

The Flash left the family and moved up the trail as fast as he dared. Luckily, the fog was thinning, so he could jog faster. However, he froze when he felt the hair on the back of his neck stand on end.

KRAK-BOOM!

The speedster dived to one side as a bolt of lightning struck the ground. Pine needles smouldered where the hero had been standing.

"I was wondering when you would show up," said a voice from above.

The Weather Wizard floated high above the treetops. The Flash could just make him out through the thinning fog. The criminal held a small wand in one hand as a swirl of wind kept him afloat. The wand allowed the villain to control the weather around him.

SCHWICK! SCHWICK!

The Weather Wizard flicked the wand and two more bolts of lightning exploded through the fog.

KRAK-KRAK! BOOM! BOOM!

The Flash didn't see the lightning bolts until the very last second. He barely dodged them as they struck the forest floor.

"Well, you may be faster than lightning after all," the villain taunted as wisps of smoke rose from charred spots left behind by the bolts.

"You'd better believe it," The Flash said.

The floating criminal grinned. "Fast enough to save yourself, maybe. But what if you have to save someone else?"

The Weather Wizard waved his wand and the fog began to clear. Little by little, the surrounding area came into sharper focus.

The Flash glanced around. The first thing he spotted was the television tower further up the mountain. It had a giant version of the Weather Wizard's wand attached to the top of it.

"So that's why you're so powerful," The Flash said.

As the fog lifted and the area cleared even more, the speedster also spotted a frightened little girl. She was huddled in a clearing further up the mountain.

The Flash didn't hesitate. In fact, he moved so fast that everything else seemed to happen in slow motion.

The Weather Wizard smirked and then flicked his wand. A bolt of lightning formed in the dark clouds above. The blinding shaft of light poked out of a cloud and then snaked down towards the girl.

The Flash raced the lightning as they both darted towards her. He pushed himself harder than ever as he swerved around trees and leapt over logs. He finally reached the girl a split second before the lightning bolt. He scooped her up just as it struck.

KRAK-BOOM!

With the girl safely in his arms, The Flash tumbled across the clearing. Then he got to his feet and sprinted down the trail.

The Weather Wizard growled to himself in frustration as he sent more lightning bolts after him.

KRAK-BOOM! KRAK-KRAK! BOOM!

The ground exploded behind the hero as the thunderbolts barely missed him. They finally let up as he ran further down the trail. A second later, he spotted the girl's parents.

The Flash quickly dropped the girl off with her family and then raced back up the mountain. As soon as the Weather Wizard came back into view, the villain sent more lightning strikes the hero's way.

KRAK·BOOM! KRAK·BOOM!

The Flash easily dodged the blasts. Then he ran up the trunk of a tall tree, trying to get close to the criminal.

"Hey! That's cheating," the Weather Wizard said.

With a flick of the villain's wrist, a bolt of lightning struck the base of the tree. As the tree exploded into splinters, The Flash lost his footing and tumbled to the ground.

"Forget it, Flash," said the criminal. "With my new Weather Wand, I'm too powerful, even for you."

The Weather Wizard raised both hands and the wind swirled around him. Soon, three tornadoes appeared nearby. They churned up the forest floor and ripped up trees as they thundered towards the hero.

"It's time to fight fire with fire," said The Flash. "Or . . . weather with weather."

The hero ran in a circle, just as he did when he unravelled the tornado in the city. Except this time, he wasn't getting rid of a twister, he was creating one of his own! The Fastest Man Alive became a red blur as he zoomed round and round. In no time, a large funnel sprouted around him before towering over the treetops.

"Hey!" snarled the Weather Wizard. "That's my routine!" The criminal waved his wand, and his three tornadoes moved faster towards the new one.

WHOOSH! WHOOSH! WHOOSH!

The Flash moved his tornado up the mountain, dodging the other twisters. He aimed it at the large antenna and pushed it ahead of him. The high winds tore at the structure, twisting it as if it were made of aluminium foil.

"No!" shouted the villain as he floated closer the structure.

The Flash's tornado tore down the tower and flung the giant weather wand free. The large rod spun through the air before slamming into the Weather Wizard. The criminal dropped his wand and plummeted to the ground.

The Flash zipped over and caught the wand in one hand and the Weather Wizard in the other. The criminal was out cold.

Suddenly, the tornadoes dissolved into nothing more than small breezes. The last of the fog disappeared and the sky cleared. The sun shone down on Central City once again.

"Looks like we're finally in for some nice weather," The Flash said. He glanced down at the unconscious criminal. "Maybe you can enjoy the view from your new cell at Blackgate Prison."

Weather Wizard

REAL NAME: Mark Mardon

OCCUPATION: Professional Criminal

HEIGHT: 1.85 metres

WEIGHT: 83 kilograms

EYES: Blue

HAIR: Grey

POWERS/ABILITIES: Flight and the ability to generate and control weather using his weather wand. He also has the ability to use various natural elements as deadly weapons, including hail, lightning and other destructive forms of weather.

BIOGRAPHY:

One night, while running from the law, Mark Mardon hid out at his brother's house. Clyde Mardon, a brilliant scientist, had just developed a device to control the Earth's weather. He planned to use this weather wand for good, but never got the chance. That night, the siblings fought, and Clyde died. No one knows if the death was accidental. But Mark fled, stealing the weather wand and using the device to continue his life of crime.

- Clyde Mardon originally built the weather wand for a super hero, but nobody knows who. Now in Mark's hands, the device allows the Weather Wizard to instantly whip up raging blizzards, powerful tornadoes, super-dense fog and other dangerous weather phenomena to commit crimes.

- The Weather Wizard's stormy wrath is usually focused on The Flash's home town of Central City — but not always. The cunning super-villain once held the entire state of Wyoming hostage with extreme weather.

- The Weather Wizard often joins forces with The Flash's other main villains. This group, known as the Rogues, includes Captain Cold, Mirror Master, Heat Wave, Trickster and Captain Boomerang.

BIOGRAPHIES

Author

Michael Anthony Steele has been in the entertainment industry for more than 27 years, writing for television, movies and video games. He has authored more than 120 books for exciting characters and brands, including Batman, Superman, Wonder Woman, Spider-Man, Shrek, Scooby-Doo, LEGO City, Garfield, *Winx Club*, *Night at the Museum* and *The Penguins of Madagascar*. Mr Steele lives on a ranch in Texas, USA, but he enjoys meeting his readers when he visits schools and libraries all across the United States. For more information, visit MichaelAnthonySteele.com.

Illustrator

Cartoonist **Gregg Schigiel** is the creator/author/illustrator of the superhero/fairy tale mash-up Pix graphic novels and was a regular contributor to Spongebob Comics. Outside of work, Mr Schigiel bakes prize-winning cookies, enjoys comedy and makes sure he drinks plenty of water. Learn more at greggschigiel.com.

GLOSSARY

antenna a tower or dish that sends or receives radio signals

blizzard a heavy snowstorm with strong winds

broadcast to send out a programme on TV

concentrate to think clearly and to give something your full attention

convertible a car with a top that can be put down

donation a contribution to a person or organization

fragment a small piece or part that is broken off of something

hail small balls of ice that form in thunderstorm clouds

identical exactly alike

retirement a time in life when someone has permanently left the workforce

rogue a dishonest person

tornado a violently rotating column of air that extends from a thunderstorm to the ground

DISCUSSION QUESTIONS

1. Who paid the bank robbers at the beginning of the story? What part did the robbery play in that person's overall plan?

2. Why does Captain Cold help The Flash? Do you think the hero should have trusted one of his most notorious enemies? Explain your answers.

3. Imagine you had the power to control the weather. What type of weather would you want to control the most? Why?

WRITING PROMPTS

1. If you could have one superpower, what would it be? Write a paragraph describing that power and what you could do with it. Then draw a picture of yourself using that power.

2. If you could run as fast as The Flash, where would you go? What places would you see? Write about having super-speed for a day!

3. At the end of the story, The Flash plans to take the Weather Wizard to prison. But what if the villain escapes along the way? Write another chapter describing how the Weather Wizard escapes and where he goes next.

LOOK FOR MORE
DC SUPER HERO ADVENTURES